**This book is dedicated to Luke, Clayton, Nathaniel and Amelia, my little snuggle monsters who never wanted to go to bed at night.**

Snuggle Monster™
Hide & Seek Bedtime™
Turn the Struggle into a Snuggle™…

Author: Greg Hughes
Illustrations: Power Kid Design & Development

Published in the United States by Continuum Games, Inc., Indianapolis, Indiana
Manufactured in Ningbo, China

Acknowledgements:
Phil Albritton
Angelika Kremer
Jon Rappoport
Wayne Rothschild

ISBN: 978-1-7337866-0-7   FIRST EDITION

www.snugglemonster.com

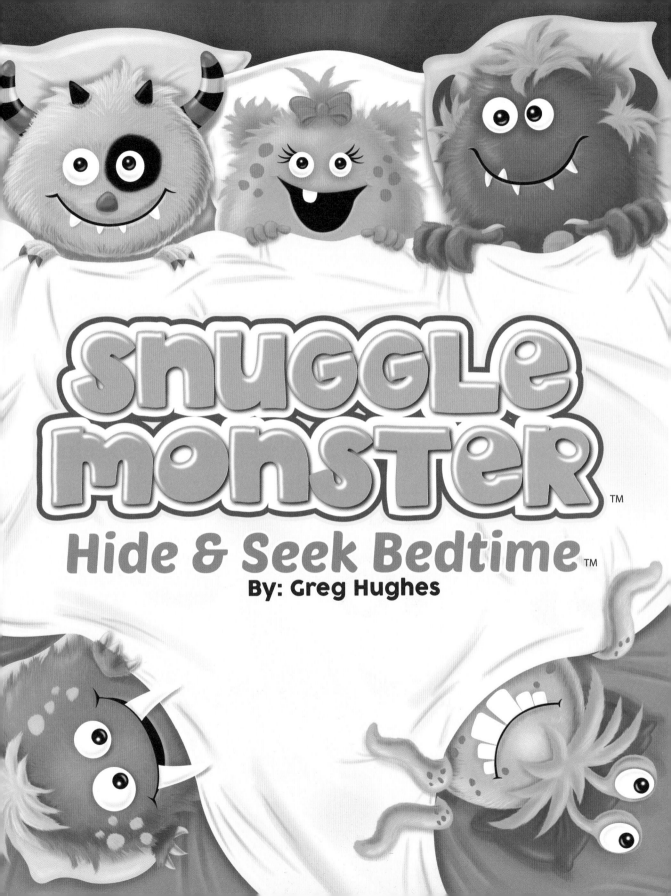

# Snuggle Monster

## Hide & Seek Bedtime ™

By: Greg Hughes

Do you know why monsters
only come out at night?
They're super silly creatures
that are afraid of the light.

Their eyes are built for nighttime.
They can't see when it's bright,
So sunshine feels like dark to them
and only gives them fright

So when the sun comes up
and it's the start of a new day,
they need to find a place to hide
before they lose their way.

They hurry and they scurry
and they hide themselves away
Then wait and wait for night to come,
when monsters like to play.

These silly, frilly monsters
want you to bring them cheer
To find them when it's bedtime
and let them know the coast is clear.

They might have horns or silly teeth,
And some are super hairy.
But you should know before you go,
These monsters? They're not scary.

You have a monster all your own
Who wants to play a game.
It starts with an introduction,
You get to give him a name.

My cute, cuddly, silly, frilly, funny, goofy,
friendly monster's name is...

Now off to your bedroom,
it's time to move along.
Each night you have to find your monster
and remember to sing this song.

Is your Snuggle Monster
Hanging out beneath your bed?
Does he have multicolored horns
Of blue and black and red?

Is he feeling hungry
Or has he been fed?
Is your Snuggle Monster
Underneath your bed?

Is that your Snuggle Monster
Hiding behind the closet door?
With goofy eyes and fur that's green
And teeth down to the floor?

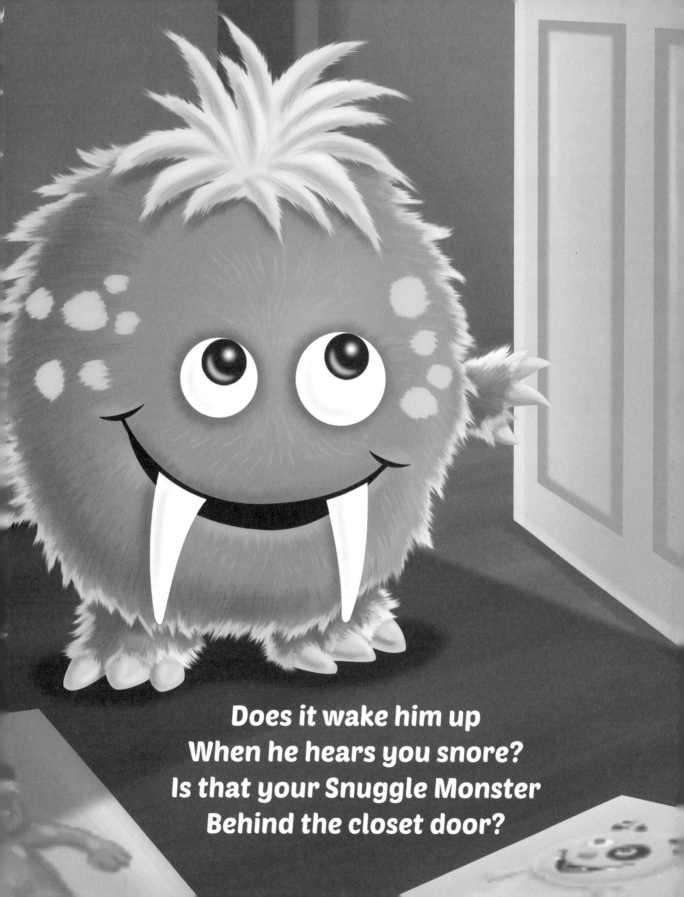

Does it wake him up
When he hears you snore?
Is that your Snuggle Monster
Behind the closet door?

If you flip the light on,
Would he dash out of sight?
Is that your Snuggle Monster
Hanging from the light?

Is that your Snuggle Monster
Chilling in your drawer?
Don't let that monster eat your socks.
Socks make monsters roar!

Is he trying on your pajamas,
so big that they tore?
Is that your Snuggle Monster
In your dresser drawer?

Is that a pink puff Snuggle Monster
in your pillowcase?
When you close your eyes
does she look you in the face?

If you were to run away,
would she give you chase?
Is that a pink puff Snuggle Monster
in your pillowcase?

Is there a Snuggle Monster underneath your bed?
Or is that monster, just made up in your head?

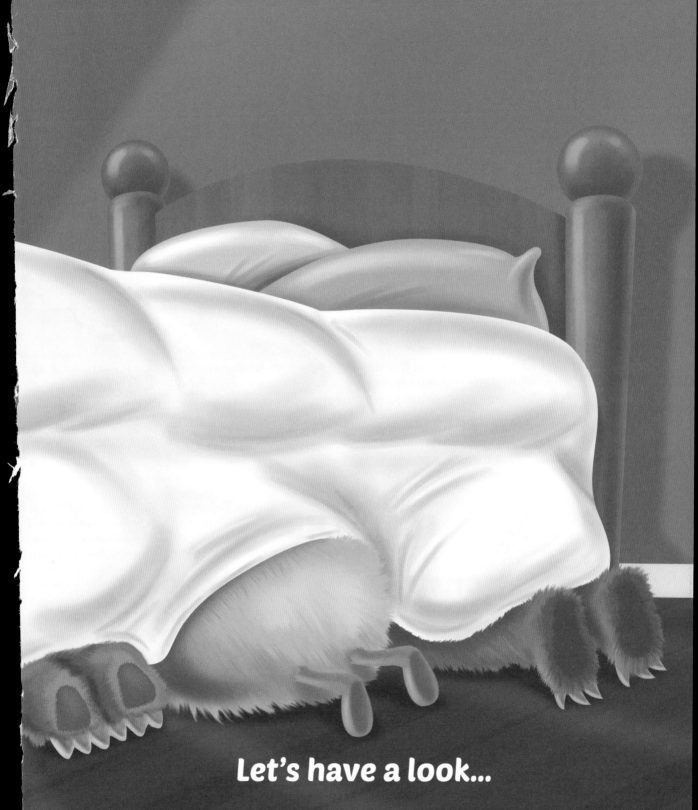

**Let's have a look...**

**FOUND HIM!**

Your monster's cute and cuddly,
Now, you know what to do.

Lights out, snuggle up
Sleep well, monsters, both of you.